© 皮皮與波西：超級滑板車

文圖　阿克賽爾・薛弗勒
譯者　酪梨壽司
責任編輯　倪若喬
美術設計　林易儒

發行人　劉振強
發行所　三民書局股份有限公司
　　　　地址　臺北市復興北路386號
　　　　電話　(02)25006600
　　　　郵撥帳號　0009998-5
門市部　(復北店) 臺北市復興北路386號
　　　　(重南店) 臺北市重慶南路一段61號
出版日期　初版四刷　2019年1月
編號　S 858121
行政院新聞局登記證局版臺業字第○二○○號

有著作權・不准侵害

ISBN　978-957-14-6107-6　（精裝）

http://www.sanmin.com.tw　三民網路書店

阿皮爾愛發明

超級滑板車

阿克賽爾·薛弗勒／文圖　酪梨壽司／譯

nosy crow

三民書局

皮皮騎著他的滑板車。

他騎上坡……

他騎下坡……

他甚至還會耍特技。

這時，波西西來了。

波西真的好喜歡皮皮的溜滑板車。

她超想一騎看。

於是波西一把撿起滑板車，有多快騎多快！

皮ㄆㄧˊ皮ㄆㄧˊ氣ㄑㄧˋ炸ㄓㄚˋ了ㄌㄜ。

波西從來沒有騎過滑板車，但她覺得那看起來很簡單。

她騎上坡……

她騎下坡……

小心！波西！

她甚至試著要特技。

波西從滑板車上摔下來。

嘘ㄛ、天ㄊㄧㄢ啊ㄚ！

可ㄎㄜˇ憐ㄌㄧㄢˊ的ㄉㄜ˙波ㄅㄛ西ㄒㄧ！

她跌傷了膝蓋，非常傷心。

皮皮為波西包紮受傷的膝蓋。

「對不起，皮皮，我不該搶走你的滑板車，」波西說。

「謝謝你照顧我。」

皮皮與波西給彼此——個大大的擁抱。

他們改去柔軟的沙坑玩沙。

最後「一起回家
吃點心。

Pip was riding on his scooter.

Just then, Posy appeared.

He went up . . .

he went down . . .

he even did tricks on it.

So Posy snatched the scooter and scooted away as fast as she could!

Pip felt **very** cross.

Posy really liked Pip's scooter.

She wanted to ride on it a lot.

Posy had never been on a scooter before, but she thought it looked quite easy.

She went **up** . . .

she went **down** . . .

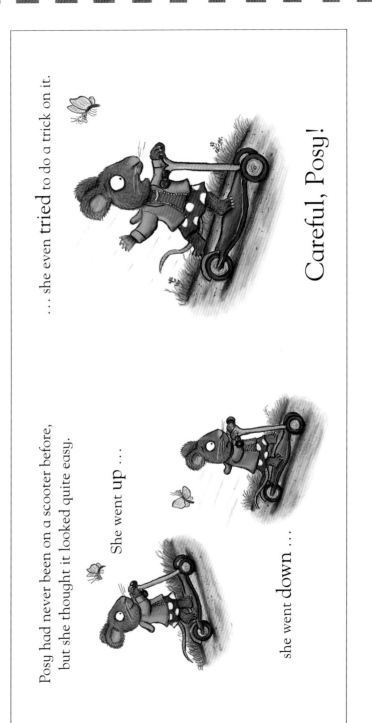

. . . she even **tried** to do a trick on it.

Careful, Posy!

Then Posy fell off the scooter.

Poor Posy!

Oh dear!

She hurt her knee and was very sad.

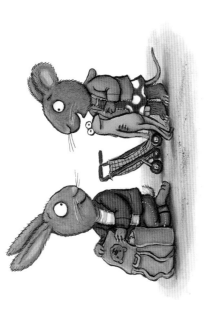

So Pip looked after Posy and her sore leg.

"I'm sorry for taking your scooter, Pip," said Posy.

"Thank you for looking after me."

Pip and Posy had a big hug.

And then they went
home for tea.

Hooray!

They went to play in the sand

where it was nice and soft.

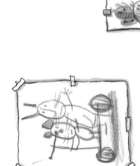

阿克賽爾‧薛弗勒　Axel Scheffler

1957年出生於德國漢堡市，25歲時前往英國就讀巴斯巴斯藝術學院。他的插畫風格幽默又不失優雅，最著名的當屬《古飛樂》(Gruffalo) 系列作品，不僅榮獲英國多項繪本大獎，譯作超過40種語言，還曾改編為動畫，深受全球觀眾喜愛，是世界知名的繪本作家。薛弗勒現居英國，持續創作中。

酪梨壽司

畢業於新聞系，擔任媒體記者數年後，前往紐約攻讀企管碩士，回臺後曾任職外商公司行銷部門。婚後旅居日本東京，目前是全職媽媽兼自由撰稿人，出沒於臉書專頁「酪梨壽司」與個人部落格「酪梨壽司的日記」。

作者簡介

譯者簡介